Walt Disney's

The Sorcerer's Apprentice

Storybook AND Magic Tricks

Retold by Teddy Slater • Illustrated by Franc Mateu
Magic Tricks by Bob Friedhoffer • Drawings by Richard Kaufman

Disney PRESS

NEW YORK

Printed and bound in the United States of America.
For information address Disney Press,
114 Fifth Avenue, New York, New York 10011

First Edition
1 3 5 7 9 10 8 6 4 2

Library of Congress Catalog Card Number: 91-73813
ISBN: 1-56282-144-X

Walt Disney's

The Sorcerer's Apprentice

Storybook AND Magic Tricks

L ong ago in a long-lost land there lived a man of magic. He was known far and wide as the Sorcerer. All the powers of the world were at his command: fire, water, wind, and earth. With a few magic words and a wave of his hand, the Sorcerer could turn dust into diamonds and diamonds into stars. He excelled at potions and magic spells. In short, there was nothing he could not do.

Night and day, the Sorcerer studied his craft. He read all the great volumes of alchemy and pyromancy, incantations and revelations. The Sorcerer was so busy with his studies and spells that he had no time at all for life's daily doings. Yet there was always the fire to be tended, the vat to be filled.

One day as the Sorcerer was looking about for his magic hat, a young lad named Mickey appeared at the door. While the Sorcerer impatiently rummaged through his things, Mickey begged to be taken on as an apprentice.

"I have no time to teach you tricks," the Sorcerer muttered as he continued his search. "As you can see, I have more than enough to do here."

The Sorcerer was just about to send him on his way when Mickey whisked a red silk scarf off a long wooden table. There beneath it was the Sorcerer's magic hat.

"Is this what you are looking for?" Mickey inquired, and it was then that the Sorcerer realized he could indeed use a bright young apprentice.

The Sorcerer's apprentice dreamed of making great magic of his own, and he begged his master to teach him how. "All in good time," the Sorcerer told him. "But first you must bring order to this chaos." And he looked with dismay at the mess all around him.

Mickey soon set to work—sweeping and swabbing, cleaning and uncluttering. But no matter how much he swept or swabbed, cleaned or uncluttered, there was always more to be done.

Sometimes Mickey would sneak away from his chores and hide behind a bureau to watch the Sorcerer at work. How he longed to be like the old man, with his tremendous powers and vast knowledge of spells. Mickey imagined that someday he, too, would don a fabulous tall hat like the Sorcerer's and create masterful illusions of his own.

Late one night the Sorcerer wearily removed his magic hat, placed it on the table, and turned toward the steep flight of stairs that led to his bedchamber.

"When you've filled the vat with water from the fountain, then you, too, may go to bed," he told Mickey, just as he told him every night. And before climbing the stairs, he pointed toward two wooden buckets in a corner of the room.

"It will be done," Mickey said obediently, although he couldn't help himself from noticing the Sorcerer's tall hat resting on the table. And no sooner was the Sorcerer out of sight than Mickey picked up the hat and put it on—just to see how it fit.

The minute the hat was on his head, Mickey felt a strange surge of power. Suddenly the Sorcerer's apprentice knew that he, too, could turn dust into diamonds. Certainly he'd seen the Sorcerer do it often enough. Unfortunately, Mickey had just finished cleaning, and there was barely a speck of dust to be seen.

Perhaps he'd try something different. . . . A sea serpent in the vat would be nice. Of course, he'd never actually seen the Sorcerer do that, but he had seen him pull a fiery dragon out of thin air. Surely a serpent would be no more difficult. But Mickey had not filled the vat, and it was bone-dry.

Mickey's eyes darted eagerly around the dimly lit cavern until they came to rest on a long, thin object lying in the far corner. On closer inspection it turned out to be nothing more than an old straw broom. But magic, after all, was magic—and the Sorcerer's apprentice had to start somewhere. Besides, he was pretty sure he knew a way to put that lowly broom to great use.

Mickey rolled up his sleeves, flung out his arms, and wriggled his fingers in the direction of the broom. Taking a deep breath, he began chanting in a voice that sounded almost exactly like the Sorcerer's very own. *"Dooma, dooma, brooma, brooma. . . ."*

There was a long moment of pure silence and stillness. And then the broom began to glow—first blue, then red, then gold. Mickey grinned with delight as it slowly came to life, sprouting two arms of its own—and then two legs.

With a grand flourish, Mickey motioned for the enchanted broom to pick up the two buckets and follow him to the fountain in the courtyard. There he directed the broom to fill the two buckets with water and carry them back to the vat.

As soon as the broom emptied the water into the vat, the Sorcerer's apprentice waved it back to the courtyard to fetch some more. The buckets were small, and the vat was deep— it would take more than a few trips to fill it to the Sorcerer's satisfaction.

Mickey watched as the broom once again scooped two buckets of water from the fountain, poured them into the vat, and headed back out to the courtyard. Then, quite pleased with himself, he settled back in the Sorcerer's big

chair to enjoy a few minutes rest, leaving the spellbound broom to finish his work.

Mickey soon fell asleep to the soothing sound of water splashing into the vat. And before he knew it, he was dreaming of softly splashing seas. . . .

In his dream, Mickey slowly ascended to the very top of a towering pinnacle. Above him was a starry sky; below, a silken sea. And there, from his lofty perch, the Sorcerer's apprentice boldly commanded the elements.

With a flutter of his fingers, Mickey made the shooting stars circle around his head like a crown of fire. Then he leaned over the water and summoned the tides to him.

First there came a gentle plume of spray, then a froth of foam. Then wave after wave came crashing across the pinnacle, higher and higher, with each flutter of Mickey's hand.

Mickey could feel his heart beating to the rhythm of the pounding surf. The stars were falling all around him like a summer rain. The waves were lapping at his feet. . . .

He awoke with a start. He was back in the Sorcerer's chair, waist-high in water. The broom was still carrying water from the fountain to the vat. No sooner did it toss two bucketfuls into the vat than it marched slowly but purposefully back outside for more. Mickey had no idea how long he'd slept, but it was clear that the vat had long since been filled. He watched in horror as the water came cascading over the rim.

"Stop!" Mickey cried. "Halt!" But the broom neither heard nor heeded. In a panic, Mickey racked his brain for the proper words to break the spell. But what little magic he knew had completely deserted him. He looked around for the Sorcerer's great book of incantations, but it was nowhere to be found.

And so the broom marched on: from the fountain, down the stairs, to the vat, and back again. Over and over, time and again, it did exactly as Mickey had bid it.

In desperation, Mickey picked up an ax that was lying on the floor, swung it high over his head, and brought it down upon the broom. *Crack!* Again and again he swung the ax until the broom lay in a pile of splinters on the ground.

Satisfied, Mickey dusted off his hands and shut the door behind him. Exhausted from his efforts, he plopped down on the ground, leaned his back against the door, and breathed a great sigh of relief.

But at that very minute, just behind the door, each of the splinters was beginning to glow—first blue, then red, then gold. An arm sprouted here, a leg sprouted there. Soon there was an army of brooms, each with two arms, each with two legs—and each with two buckets! All at once, and all together, the vast army of brooms started to march.

Mickey felt a vibration in the floor beneath him and opened the door a crack to peek outside. A parade of brooms was coming toward him! He pulled the door shut and threw

his weight against it. But the Sorcerer's apprentice was no match for the army of brooms. Four abreast, in a column as far as the eye could see, they trampled right over him.

As the brooms steadily poured more and more water into the vat, Mickey frantically began to bail the water out a nearby window. But it was no use. For every bucket he managed to bail out, each of the brooms poured in two more.

As the floodwaters rose around him, Mickey felt himself being dragged down, down, down. Gasping for air, he struggled to the surface only to be battered down by the towering waves.

Whirling and swirling, the water swept Mickey off his feet and carried him along in its current.

Once again the waters closed over his head, and Mickey reached out desperately for something to hang on to. Just then, as luck would have it, the Sorcerer's great book of incantations went drifting by.

Mickey scrambled aboard the big book as if it were a life raft and frantically riffled through its pages, searching for the right spell to undo the damage. But the current was fierce, and within seconds he was sucked into a whirlpool and spun around and around and back down into the watery depths.

Suddenly a beam of white light pierced the darkness. Mickey looked up, and there, on the stairs, stood his master.

Slowly the Sorcerer raised his arms. Then, murmuring words only he could hear, he thrust both arms straight out, fingers pointing to the terrible torrent. Suddenly the raging sea parted, and the waters began to recede.

And when the last swirl of water had vanished, there Mickey stood, wet and shivering, in a shallow puddle. As he gazed up sheepishly, the Sorcerer gazed down at him with cold, angry eyes.

While the Sorcerer continued to stare sternly, Mickey took off the magic hat and returned it to its owner. Then he picked up the two water buckets and, with downcast eyes, started off to complete his chores. And so he never even saw the sly little smile the Sorcerer flashed as he picked up the once-enchanted broom and swept his apprentice off his feet and out the door.

But from then on, the Sorcerer somehow found a few minutes at the end of each day to teach his pupil the true uses of magic. It wasn't long before the eager apprentice knew almost as much as his master. And just to make sure he would not forget a single trick or spell, Mickey wrote everything down in his own big book of magic.

Walt Disney's

The Sorcerer's Apprentice

BOOK OF MAGIC

Table of Contents

1

How to Make a Magic Wand

Before you start making magic, you may want to make a magic wand. Magic wands are not just for show. Sometimes you can use a magic wand to point at things, to make a point, or to distract your audience while you perform some sleight of hand. A magic wand can be a long, straight stick that you find outside, a pencil, a ruler, or even a wooden spoon. But if you want to make a traditional wand, follow these simple directions.

PROPS

a 12-inch-long round, wooden stick (between ¼"
   and ½" in diameter)
black paint
white paint
a paintbrush

Paint the entire stick black, and let the paint dry. Then paint each end white. The white paint should cover about 1 inch of each tip.

The Mysterious Multiplying Cards

THE EFFECT

After showing the audience that you have six cards in your hand, you throw away three cards and still wind up with six!

PROPS

a deck of cards
transparent tape
a pair of scissors

SETUP

For this trick the secret is in the "envelope card." To make the envelope card, you need two cards. Cut off the upper-right-hand corner of one of the cards as shown in illustration #1. Tape the cut card to the back of the uncut card (illustration #2). The face of the cut card should touch the back of the uncut card. You now have an "envelope." Take three cards from the deck and place them all facedown, inside the envelope. Take five more cards from the deck, and you're ready to perform the trick.

Arrange the cards as follows:

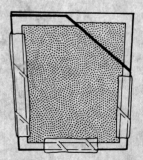

1.

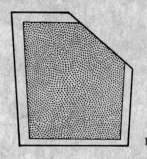

2.

Put the five plain cards on the table, facedown, one on top of the other. Place the envelope card facedown on top of the plain cards. The cut portion of the envelope card should be in the upper-right-hand corner. Pick up the cards.

ROUTINE AND METHOD

Begin by saying, "With these magic cards, I will now prove that six minus three equals six. Let me show you what I mean."

Hold the cards, faces to the audience, in your left hand and count them one at a time into your right hand.

Take the card from the rear (the envelope card) in your right hand first, then the next card, placing it on the face of the envelope card, and so on, counting the cards out loud. They should still be in their original order, with the envelope card at the back. Return all the cards to your left hand, pause a moment, and say:

"I can take away three cards—like so." This time, remove the cards from *inside* the envelope card, as shown in illustration #3, and count, "One, two, three." Put these cards on the table.

Next, count out the remaining cards, including the envelope card, into your right hand, just as you did the first time, showing that you still have six cards left!

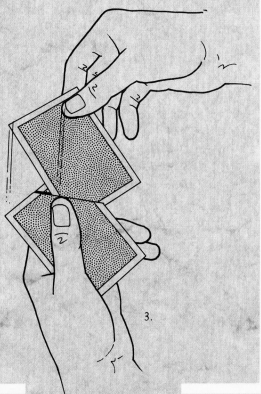

3.

Black Card—Red Card

THE EFFECT

Two cards—one red, one black—magically change places.

PROPS

the 3 of hearts
the jack of clubs
two playing cards of any suit
glue

SETUP

Glue together the 3 of hearts and the jack of clubs, back-to-back. Then glue together the other two cards, face-to-face. Place the cards under a flat, heavy weight—like a stack of books—while they dry, to make sure they don't curl up. When they are dry, you'll have one double-faced playing card and one double-backed card.

ROUTINE AND METHOD

Hold the cards in your left hand as shown in illustration #1. It will look as if you are holding two normal cards, one faceup and the other facedown.

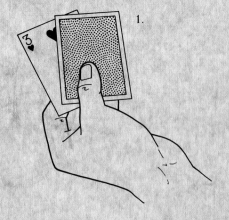

Now say, "In my hand are two cards: the 3 of hearts"—then turn your hand over—"and the jack of clubs" (illustration #2).

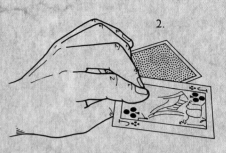

Turn your hand over, back and forth, two or three times, showing both sides of the prepared cards.

Tell your friends, "Watch carefully. I'm going to put the 3 of hearts behind my back." As you do this, take the double-faced card with the 3 of hearts facing the audience and slowly bring it behind your back. (The double-backed card should still be in your left hand.) Then add, "That means that this remaining card is the jack of clubs." Then say, "*Alakazoo, alakazam*. The two cards will now change places." As you are saying this, turn over the card behind your back so when you bring it back out in front of you, it will show the jack of clubs. Place the two cards together one more time. The audience will be surprised, expecting that the jack of clubs was the facedown card they'd been watching all along!

Show both cards again, just as you did at the beginning of the trick. You can either do the trick a second time or put the cards away. It's not a good idea to let the audience examine the cards!

4

The Disappearing Dime

THE EFFECT

A dime placed in the middle of a handkerchief magically vanishes into thin air.

PROPS

a dime
a large handkerchief
(bandannas are perfect)
a magic wand

ROUTINE AND METHOD

Lay the handkerchief out, flat on the table, and hold up the dime. Now say, "Watch carefully as I take this coin, lay it in the middle of the handkerchief, and make it disappear."

Put the coin in the center and fold the handkerchief *exactly* as shown in illustrations #1–4. Ask a volunteer to tap the handkerchief lightly with the magic wand while you say your favorite magic words.

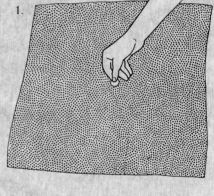

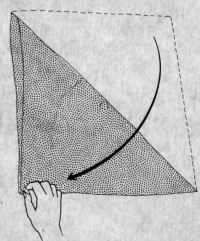

26

Holding the corners of the handkerchief as shown in illustration #5, lift the handkerchief off the table and pull slowly. The coin will seem to disappear, although it will actually remain hidden in the fold of the handkerchief (illustration #6). If you've done this carefully, your audience will not be able to see it.

Note: Make sure there is no light behind you when you do this trick.

5

The Reappearing Dime

THE EFFECT

The dime that disappeared in the last trick materializes in an empty matchbox.

PROPS

another dime
a small, empty matchbox
a magic wand

SETUP

Open the matchbox halfway. Wedge the dime between the cover of the box and the top of the drawer as shown in the illustration.

ROUTINE AND METHOD

Hold up the matchbox and carefully turn it upside down to show that it is empty. Then turn the box right side up and close it. The wedged dime should fall into the drawer of the box without your audience hearing it.

Place the box on the table and say, "With your assistance, I will now use my magic powers to bring back the dime I made vanish in the last trick."

Ask a volunteer to tap the matchbox lightly with the magic wand and say the magic words, *"Ramalama gamalama!"* Then ask the volunteer to open the matchbox. He or she will be amazed to discover that the vanishing coin has reappeared.

6

The Invisible Knife

THE EFFECT
A banana is miraculously sliced into three pieces—before it is peeled.

PROPS
a banana
a sewing needle

SETUP
Before your audience arrives, insert the needle through the skin of the banana and into the fruit, about one-third of the way from the top. Wiggle the needle back and forth, slicing the fruit inside while leaving the skin in one piece (except for a tiny pinhole).

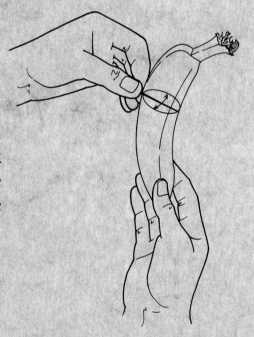

Repeat this procedure, but this time insert the needle one-third of the way from the bottom of the banana.

ROUTINE AND METHOD
Holding your right hand up as if holding a knife, say, "In this hand is an invisible knife."

Then hold up the precut banana in your left hand and

add, "This knife is so sharp that it can cut the inside of a banana without cutting the skin!"

Place the banana on a table and make a cutting motion with the invisible knife. As your audience looks on in disbelief, announce, "Watch—I'll do it again."

After you make the second "cut," ask someone to peel the banana, and show that it has been sliced into three pieces.

7

Double Your Money

THE EFFECT
Money multiplies in a friend's hands.

PROPS

a hardcover book
a 6″ × ½″ strip of thin cardboard
15–20 assorted coins (nickels, dimes, and pennies)
a magic wand

SETUP

Open the book somewhere near the middle. Place the cardboard strip in the center of the book, like you would a bookmark. The cardboard should not stick out when the book is closed. Place four coins next to the cardboard strip as shown in illustration #1. Then gently close the book.

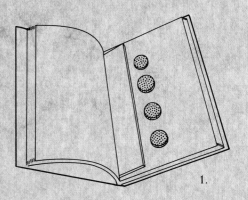

1.

ROUTINE AND METHOD

Announce to your audience: "I can actually make money by magic!"

Take some coins out of your pocket and hand them to an audience member. Then open the book to a place about

31

10 or 15 pages *before* the page with the cardboard and say, "I want you to place these coins on this page, then tell us how much money there is."

After the money has been counted and placed on the page, ask the volunteer to cup their hands together and hold them out.

Say the magic word, *"Abraca-dabra!"* and tilt the book so that *all* of the money falls into their hands (illustration #2). Tap their hands gently with your magic wand and say, "I want you to count the money again."

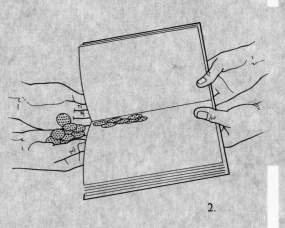

2.

When they do, they will be amazed to find that the money has multiplied!

Of course, what they don't know is that the coins hidden next to the cardboard strip have also fallen into their hands.

8

The Magically Restored String

THE EFFECT
A length of string is cut in two, and the two pieces are magically rejoined.

PROPS
a piece of multistrand, solid-color cotton string,
    like the kind used in a bakery
glue
scissors

SETUP
Take a 12-inch length of string and carefully glue the ends together so it looks like a solid, unbroken circle.

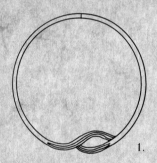

At a point opposite the glued ends, separate the strands of the string into two even groups as shown in illustration #1. Make the separation about 3 inches long.

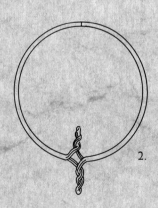

Take each group of strands and twist in the center as shown in illustration #2. The twisted strands should appear to be criss-crossing ends of string. Anyone seeing the string will be fooled into thinking that the twisted parts are the *ends* of the string.

ROUTINE AND METHOD
Point to the set-up string lying on the table. Then pick it up by the twisted strands that look like the ends (illustration #3). Say to the audience, "I will now cut an ordinary piece of string in half."

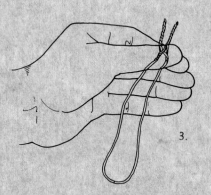

3.

Take the scissors and cut the string in the place that you glued it together so it *looks* as if you cut the middle of the string and are now holding two pieces of string as shown in illustration #4.

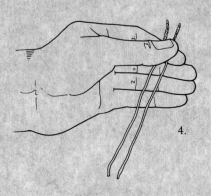

4.

Close your hand into a loose fist around the twisted ends, allowing the ends you just cut to hang down as shown in illustration #5. Ask someone from your audience to grab both of the hanging ends—one in each hand—and pull slowly away from your fist. When that person has pulled the string until it's taut, open your fist. The twisted strands will have been pulled back into their original position, and it will seem as though the string has been magically restored!

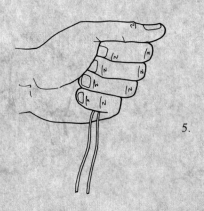

5.

9

Going, Going, Gone

THE EFFECT
A coin disappears with no gimmicks—just some real sleight of hand.

PROPS
a borrowed coin

SETUP
To do this trick, you must be wearing a shirt that is tucked in.

ROUTINE AND METHOD
Borrow a coin from someone in your audience and say, "Watch carefully as I make this coin vanish by rubbing it into my elbow."

Put your left elbow on the table as shown in illustration #1. Make sure your left hand is resting near your neck, by your shirt collar.

1.

Hold the borrowed coin in your right fingertips and start to rub it against your left elbow. After a few seconds, let it "accidentally" drop to the tabletop and say, "Uh-oh! Let me try that again."

Pick up the coin with your *left* hand, grab it with your right fingertips, and start to rub it against your left elbow again. Your elbow should be back on the table in the same position as before.

Drop the coin a second time and pretend it was an accident again.

Pick it up with your left hand one more time. But now just *pretend* to transfer the coin from your left hand to your right. You should actually keep it hidden in your left hand as shown in illustration #2.

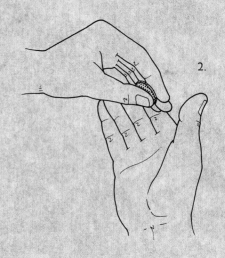

Put your left elbow back on the table, and put your left hand—which is secretly holding the coin—near your shirt collar for the last time.

Start rubbing the "coin" against your left elbow and, while everyone is watching, secretly drop the real coin that is in your left hand inside your shirt collar and down your shirt as shown in illustration #3.

After a few moments, open up your empty right hand and say, "Voilà! The coin has vanished!"

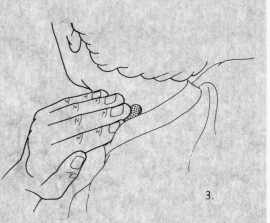

X Marks the Spot

THE EFFECT
A straight line drawn on your friend's hand mysteriously turns into crisscrossing lines.

PROPS
a piece of chalk (soft chalk works best)

ROUTINE AND METHOD
Tell your friend, "I will make a magic mark on the palm of your hand with a piece of ordinary chalk." Using the chalk, draw a thin straight line on your friend's palm exactly as shown in illustration #1.

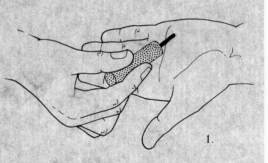

Next tell your friend to study the mark, then close their hand into a tight fist. Make some motions with your hands in front of their face and say your favorite magic words.

Now ask, "What did I draw on your hand?"

They should say, "A straight line."

Then you say, "Open your hand and take a look."

When they open their hand, they will be shocked to see an X on their palm instead of a straight line! (Illustration #2.)

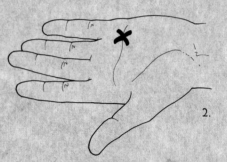

Your friend will think you're a fine magician, but actually they've done most of the work. When they folded their hand into a fist, the skin on either side of the wrinkle that you drew across was pressed together. Some of the chalk from the drawn line transferred to the clean skin, "magically" forming an X.

11

The Unbreakable Toothpick

THE EFFECT

With a wave of your magic wand, a broken toothpick is made whole again.

PROPS

a supply of toothpicks
a bandanna
a magic wand

SETUP

Have an adult sew a small pocket, about 4 inches long, at one corner of the bandanna as shown in illustration #1. Conceal a toothpick in the pocket.

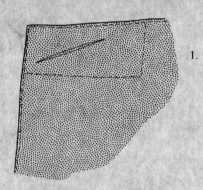
1.

ROUTINE AND METHOD

Bring out the bandanna, open it up, and lay it flat on the table. Have a volunteer from the audience select a toothpick from your supply and hand it to you. Take the toothpick with your right hand and pretend to place it under the center of the bandanna, but don't actually let it out of your hand. As you pretend to place the toothpick under the bandanna, take the corner with the concealed toothpick and push it under the center of the bandanna, as shown in illustration #2, while lifting the bandanna off the table. Keep your right hand and the chosen toothpick underneath the bandanna (illustration #3).

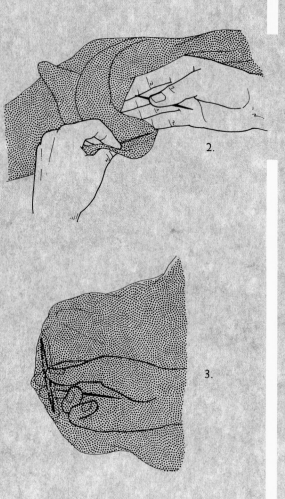

2.

3.

Ask your volunteer to feel the toothpick through the bandanna, but make sure it's the toothpick in the secret pocket that the volunteer is feeling. Have the volunteer snap the toothpick in two. He or she will both feel and hear it snap. Say a few magic words and lift the bandanna with your left hand to reveal the unbroken toothpick in your right hand! The actual broken toothpick will stay safely in its secret pocket even if you wave the bandanna around.

12

Disappearing Objects

THE EFFECT
A special bandanna is used to make ordinary objects disappear.

PROPS
two identical bandannas
scissors
needle and thread
a small object, such as a rubber ball or die

SETUP
Cut a round hole, about 4 inches in diameter, in the center of one bandanna. Ask an adult to sew around the edges of the hole so it won't fray, and then sew all four edges of both bandannas together as shown in illustration #1.

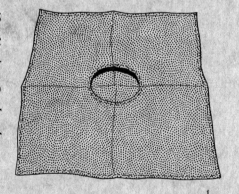

1.

ROUTINE AND METHOD
Place the small object in the palm of your left hand. Announce, "I am going to cover this with the famous Cloth of Invisibility. In just one moment, it will become invisible."

Bring the bandanna out of your pocket, and cover the object with the side that has the hole in the center. Make sure that the hole goes over the object (illustration #2) and that everyone can see the object's outline through the cloth.

Holding one corner of the bandanna with your right fingertips, quickly whisk it away from your left palm as shown in illustration #3. The object will drop inside the bandanna's secret pocket. To your audience, it will seem as though the object has vanished. Now say, "You may think it has disappeared, but it's still here. It's simply become invisible."

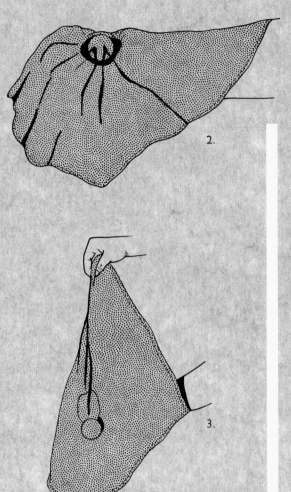

Note: With a little practice, you can make a variety of things vanish as long as they can fit inside the secret hole. And if you handle the bandanna in a natural way, no one will suspect that it's anything but a plain piece of cloth.

13

The Color-Changing Handkerchief

THE EFFECT

A white handkerchief is transformed into a red one.

PROPS

a small (9″–12″ square) white handkerchief
a small (9″–12″ square) red handkerchief
two sheets of (tabloid-size) newspaper
glue
a magic wand

SETUP

The newspaper should be prepared beforehand as follows: Glue together the two sheets of newspaper, following the glue lines as shown in illustration #1.

Crease the prepared newspaper as shown in the next illustration (#2) so you can easily form it into a cone when the proper time comes. When the glue dries, you should have two separate pockets in the newspaper. Place the red handkerchief in one of the pockets.

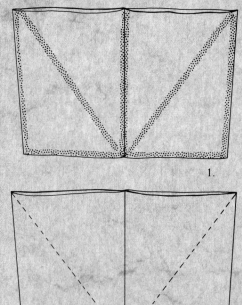

1.

2.

ROUTINE AND METHOD

For a magically mesmerizing effect, try doing this trick wordlessly to music.

Hold the newspaper in one hand and show both sides to your audience. As you fold the newspaper into a cone as shown in illustration #3, secretly open the empty pocket a bit.

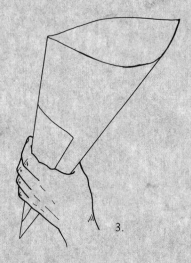

While your audience watches, place the white handkerchief into the newspaper cone, making sure that it goes inside the other, empty pocket. For effect, poke the handkerchief in all the way with your magic wand.

Still holding the newspaper in a cone shape, wave your magic wand over the top and say your favorite magic words. Then reach into the cone and remove the red handkerchief from the other secret pocket. Unfold the paper and show your audience both sides again. There will be nothing suspicious to see.

14

The Bouncing Handkerchief

THE EFFECT

A handkerchief thrown to the floor bounces right back up into your hand.

PROPS

a lightweight handkerchief
a high-bouncing ball (1"–1½" in diameter)
needle and thread

SETUP

Place the ball on one corner of the handkerchief. Fold the handkerchief over to completely cover the ball. Have an adult sew the folded corner shut, with the ball inside, as shown in illustration #1.

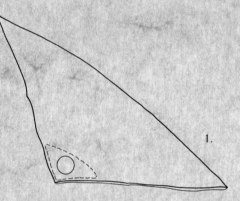

1.

ROUTINE AND METHOD

At the beginning, the prepared handkerchief should be in your pants pocket. After you've performed one of the other magic tricks in this book, take the handkerchief out of your pocket, casually use it to wipe your face, and then return it to your pocket.

Do another trick and wipe your face with the handkerchief a second time. By now the audience should have no doubt that the handkerchief is just an ordinary one.

Finally, do another trick and wipe your face again. But this time, instead of putting the handkerchief back in your pocket, throw it down on the floor (illustration #2).

Thanks to the high-bouncing ball, your handkerchief will magically bounce off the floor and back into your hand. Your audience will not believe their eyes!

15

Mind Reading

THE EFFECT
You are able to see behind your back—without looking.

PROPS
six crayons (all different colors)

ROUTINE AND METHOD

Give someone six crayons. Then put both of your hands behind your back and ask that person to select one crayon, show it to the audience—but not to you—and put it into your hands.

Now, with your hands still behind your back, scrape a little bit of the crayon under a fingernail on your right hand as shown in illustration #1. Slowly bring your right hand out in front of you, letting your friends see that it is empty. Place that same hand to your forehead as if you are concentrating deeply. As you move your hand away, take a quick glance at the color of the scraping as shown in illustration #2. Wait a few seconds, then declare the color of the crayon behind your back.

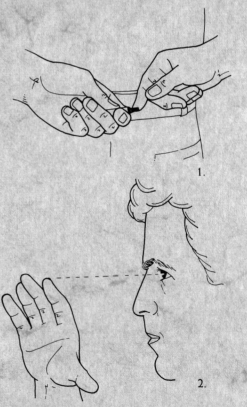

16

Crazy Spots

A flat two-sided card is shown to have four sides.

PROPS
a 6″ × 10″ piece of cardboard
a crayon or felt-tip pen

SETUP
Draw dots on both sides of the cardboard exactly as shown in illustrations #1 and #2. To make this illusion work, study illustrations #3–6 carefully in order to learn the correct way to handle the cardboard. Remember, the whole trick depends on how expertly you cover and uncover the spots as the card goes from hand to hand. After a little practice, you'll be able to do it and look natural the whole time.

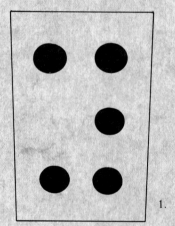

1.

2.

ROUTINE AND METHOD

Hold the card up as shown in illustration #3 and say to your audience, "You see before you a special card. It appears to have only two sides. But with a few magic words—*Hocus, pocus, dots in focus*—I'll prove that it really has four!"

As you reveal each of the different sides, announce that side 1 has six dots (illustration #3), side 2 has three dots (illustration #4), side 3 has four dots (illustration #5), and side 4 has one dot (illustration #6).

Repeat the trick one more time, then put the card away.

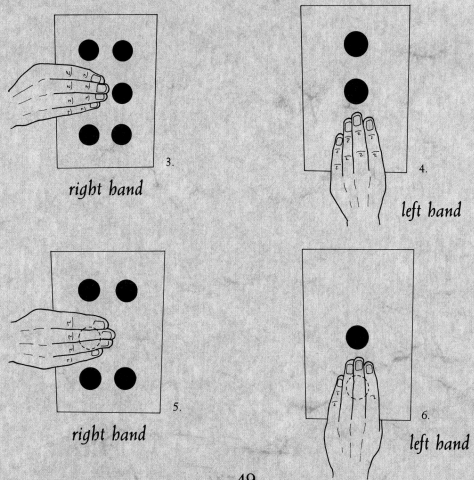

3.

right hand

4.

left hand

5.

right hand

6.

left hand

17

The Floating Pencil

THE EFFECT

A pencil mysteriously rises out of an empty soda bottle.

PROPS

a long pencil with an eraser on one end
a small empty soda bottle or juice bottle
very fine thread
a sharp knife

SETUP

You must be wearing a shirt with buttons to do this trick.

Have an adult take the knife and carefully slice down the center of the eraser, from top to bottom, as shown in illustration #1.

Tie one end of the thread around one of your shirt buttons. Tie a small knot in the free end of the thread. Slip the knotted end of the thread through the slit in the eraser as shown in illustration #2. The knot will keep the thread from being pulled out.

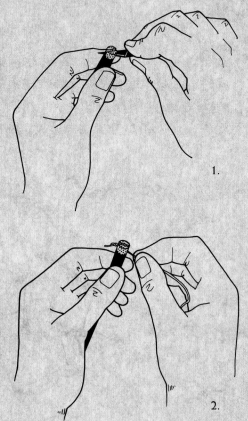

1.

2.

Hold the bottle close to your stomach with your left hand. Place the pencil in the bottle, eraser end first, with your right hand.

Proclaim, "I am going to make this pencil levitate. It will break the bonds of gravity and float through the air."

Move the bottle away from your stomach as if to give your audience a better view (illustration #3). Everyone will be astounded to see the pencil slowly levitating out of the bottle. Of course, the farther you move the bottle away from your stomach, the higher the pencil will rise. For an extra effect, wave your right hand ceremoniously above the bottle as the pencil rises.

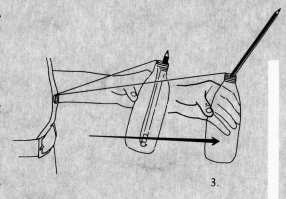

3.

At this point simply take the pencil from the bottle with your right hand and move it away from your body. Tilt the eraser toward you so the thread will slip out as you hand the pencil to a member of the audience. You may then invite them to examine both the pencil and the bottle.

18

The Enchanted Handkerchief

THE EFFECT
A coin passes through a handkerchief without leaving a hole.

PROPS
a coin
a handkerchief

ROUTINE AND METHOD

Hold the coin with your right fingertips and tell your audience, "I can make this coin pass through a handkerchief without leaving a hole in the cloth. Watch carefully." Then place the center of the handkerchief over the coin, pinching a piece of cloth behind the coin with your right thumb as shown in illustration #1.

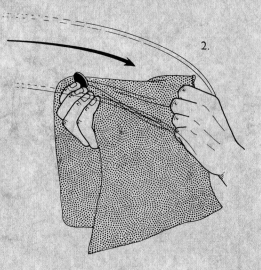
1.

Pick up the front half of the handkerchief to let the audience see the coin underneath. As you pick up the front of the handkerchief, toss it over the top of the coin so that it rests on the back half of the handkerchief as shown in illustration #2.

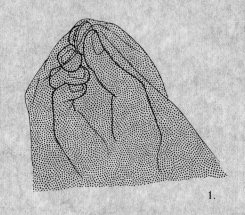
2.

When the audience has seen the coin, pull the front of the handkerchief back over the coin, bringing both the *front* and the *back* halves of the handkerchief over as shown in illustration #3, all the while making sure your right thumb is still pinching a small piece of the cloth behind the coin.

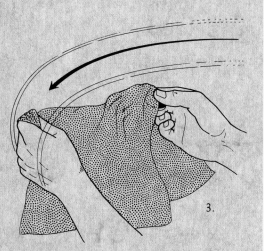

3.

Now have a volunteer grab the ends of the handkerchief and slowly pull it from your fingertips (illustration #4). If you keep a firm grasp on the coin, the handkerchief will be pulled out of your hand, but the coin will remain in your fingertips. It will seem as if the coin passed right through the cloth.

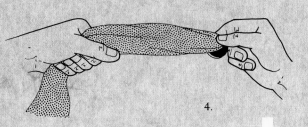

4.

19

Three in the Hand, One in the Pocket

THE EFFECT
A coin jumps invisibly from your pocket to your hand.

PROPS
five identical coins
a magic wand

ROUTINE AND METHOD
Place four of the coins and your magic wand on the table. Keep the fifth coin hidden in your right hand as shown in illustration #1. If you do this trick smoothly, your audience will not suspect that there is a fifth coin.

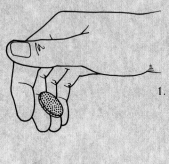

Use your right hand to slide three coins to the table's edge, one at a time, then off the edge and into your left hand. As you slide the first coin into your left hand, say, "One." When you slide the second coin into your left hand, say, "Two," but allow the extra coin, hidden in your right hand, to fall in with it (illustration #2). Slide the third coin from the

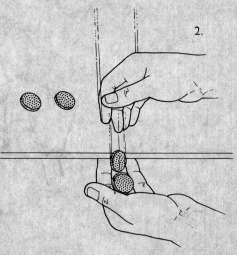

54

tabletop into your left hand and say, "Three." There will actually be four coins in your left hand, but the audience will be aware of only three.

Pick up the fourth coin from the table with your right hand and say, "I will now place the fourth coin in my pocket," and do so.

Ask your audience, "How many coins do I have in my left hand?" and wait for someone to say, "Three." Then answer, "That is correct. But now watch as I make the fourth coin jump from my pocket into my left hand."

Using your right hand, touch your magic wand to the outside of your pocket and to the back of your left hand. Say, *"Hocus pocus!"* and then open your left hand to show that it now holds four coins.

20

The Vanishing Queen

THE EFFECT

The joke is on the audience when the queen of hearts vanishes—and is replaced by a joker.

PROPS

four cards from an old deck (two black number cards, such as the 2 of clubs and the 4 of spades, a joker, and the queen of hearts)
transparent tape
scissors

SETUP

Cut the queen of hearts, diagonally, as shown in illustration #1. Tape the smaller piece to the club card, facedown, *exactly* as shown in illustration #2. Discard the other part of the queen.

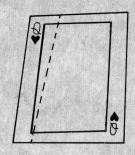

Before you perform this trick, flip the cut card over so the face of the queen is showing and slip the joker between the queen and the club card as shown in illustra-

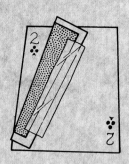

tion #3. Cover the exposed part of the joker with the spade card. Arrange the cards in a fan as shown in illustration #4 so that it looks as if the queen of hearts is surrounded by two other cards.

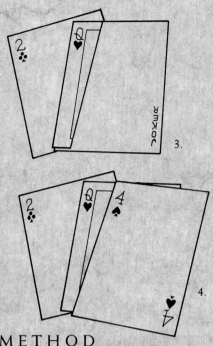

ROUTINE AND METHOD

Holding the fan of cards so that the audience can see them, announce, "I have three cards—the 2 of clubs, the queen of hearts, and the 4 of spades."

Turn the fan facedown and ask someone to point to the queen. When they point to the middle card in the fan, say, "I will now remove the queen and leave it on the table." Slide the facedown "queen" (actually the joker) from the middle of the fan and leave it facedown on the table.

Next, carefully slide the 4 of spades over the half-queen of hearts, hiding it from view. Then turn the fan faceup. The audience will see only the 2 of clubs and the 4 of spades.

If you now ask, "Where is the queen of hearts?" everyone should say, "On the table." At that point ask someone to turn over the card on the table. No one will believe their eyes when that card turns out to be the joker!

21

The Secret Saltshaker

THE EFFECT
While sitting at a table, you make a saltshaker disappear.

PROPS
  a saltshaker
  a large, thick paper napkin
  a table

ROUTINE AND METHOD
Sit at the table and cover the salt-shaker with the napkin, smoothing it down to form the shape of the saltshaker as shown in illustration #1.

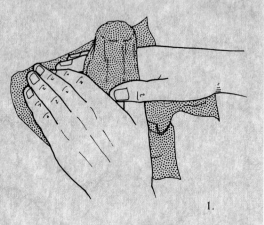

1.

Waving your hands over the saltshaker, announce, "I will now make a butterfly appear under the saltshaker."

Quickly pick up the napkin-covered saltshaker and look surprised when you don't find a butterfly. Place the shaker, still covered by the napkin, back on the table. Pick it up and put it down again, still looking puzzled.

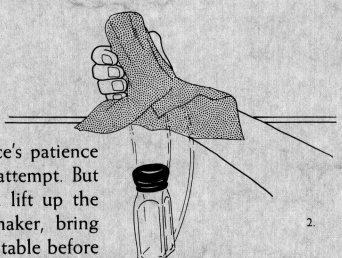

2.

Ask for your audience's patience as you begin a third attempt. But this time, when you lift up the napkin-covered saltshaker, bring it to the edge of the table before putting it down and let the salt-shaker slip silently from the nap-kin into your lap (illustration #2).

Still holding the saltshaker-shaped napkin loosely in your hand, put it back on the table in its original place. The napkin should be able to stand on its own and look as though it is still covering the saltshaker.

Wait a moment and tell your friends that you've changed your mind. Instead of making a butterfly appear, you will make the shaker *disappear*!

Slowly push down on the top of the napkin. Your au-dience will be flabbergasted when your hand crushes the napkin to reveal that the saltshaker has vanished.

Mystic Straw

THE EFFECT

A soda straw moves magically across a tabletop.

PROPS

a 4-inch section of a drinking straw, either paper or plastic

ROUTINE AND METHOD

Place the section of the straw on a smooth tabletop. Say your favorite magic words, then wave your hands over the straw as if casting a spell on it. Your hand motions should be as graceful and complicated as possible. Then, still waving your hands, quietly blow the straw across the tabletop, making the audience think the straw is moving on its own. Once the straw starts to move, it will keep rolling with only the slightest breath. Your audience will be so busy watching your hands and the straw that no one will notice what you're doing with your mouth.

The Spellbound Ring

THE EFFECT
An enchanted ring "jumps" from one finger to another finger.

PROPS
a ring

ROUTINE AND METHOD
Extend the index finger and the middle finger of your right hand. Place the ring on the end (above the knuckle) of the middle finger. It should be a snug fit.

Hold your left hand, formed into a fist, waist-high in front of your body, with the back of your hand facing up. Rest the two extended fingers of your right hand on top of your left fist as shown in illustration #1.

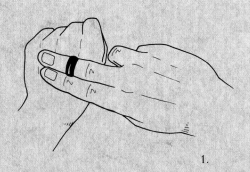

1.

Count out loud, "One ... two... three. . . ." As you count each number, raise and lower your right hand into the air about a foot. On the counts of "one" and "two," just raise the hand and return it to its resting position. But as you raise your hand on "three," close the index finger into your right hand and extend your ring finger alongside your middle finger as shown in illustration #2. Do this secretly while your whole hand is in motion. If you do it fast enough, your audience should not see one finger being closed and the other extended. It will look as if the ring has jumped from your middle finger to your index finger (illustration #3), when actually the ring hasn't moved at all!

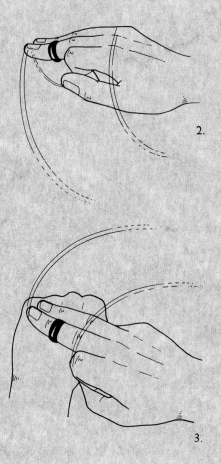

2.

3.